A Galdone Treasury

Nursery Classics

Stories and Pictures by Paul Galdone

With an introduction by Leonard S. Marcus

Clarion Books ⬥ New York

Clarion Books
a Houghton Mifflin Company imprint
215 Park Avenue South, New York, NY 10003

The text was set in 16-point ITC Century Book.
Book design by Janet Pedersen.
All rights reserved.

Printed in the USA.

Library of Congress Cataloging-in-Publication Data
Galdone, Paul.
Nursery classics : a Galdone treasury / stories and pictures by Paul Galdone ;
with an introduction by Leonard S. Marcus.
p. cm.
ISBN 0-618-13046-2
1. Tales. [1. Folklore. 2. Nursery rhymes.] I. Marcus, Leonard S., 1950– . II. Title.

PZ8.1.G15 Nu 2001
398.2—dc21

00-065599

RMT 10 9 8 7 6 5 4 3 2 1

Contents

Introduction

For Paul Galdone (1907-1986), drawing was a lifeline and a favorite way of paying attention. "Draw, draw, draw. [It was] the only thing I wanted to do [as a young person]. And I still have that same urge." When he wrote these words, the Hungarian-born artist and author was not quite seventy and the illustrator of more than 160 children's books by himself and others. Among his happiest memories of growing up in the politically volatile, sometimes violent Hungary of the 1920s were of sketching the animals at the Budapest zoo and taking art lessons that his father, a typewriter salesman and Sunday painter with an operatic voice, had arranged for him. "The smell of the oil paints," Galdone later recalled, "overwhelmed me with a desire to become an artist." He never wavered in his determination to do so.

Galdone was a teenager when his family immigrated to the United States and settled in New Jersey. High school classmates laughed at his English but marveled at his ability to draw. (Grasshoppers were a specialty.) Following graduation, he moved to New York's Greenwich Village and worked as a busboy, fur dyer, and electrician's helper and at other odd jobs while taking night classes at the Art Students League, where his teachers included the great German satirical artist George Grosz and the painter Guy Pène du Bois. Then a job at the publisher Doubleday & Company introduced Galdone to the book-related "applied" arts of design, typography, and illustration, and led to the opportunity to design a book jacket. Emboldened by the success of his first assignment, he left Doubleday and in the years before World War II set up shop in New York as a freelance designer/illustrator. Children's book work still lay more than a decade in the future. But from then onward Galdone, like the doughty heroes of "The Little Red Hen," "The Three Little Pigs," and other traditional folk stories with which he later became identified, lived by his own work and wits.

Galdone was a robust, witty, hard-working, garrulous (though fundamentally shy), sardonic, generous, down-to-earth man. He never took his talent as an artist entirely for granted. He was a romantic with a strong touch of pragmatism and an honest craftsman who gave good weight while concealing from readers the strenuous effort by which he achieved his picture books' signature illusion of carefree amiability. "I have [already] discarded 3 approaches to the 3 little pigs," he wrote his long-time editor James Cross Giblin in the summer of 1969. "Studied every [version] in the 42[nd Street] Library. . . . I don't want to produce anything resembling any of the others."

He examined plants and animals in the field with equal care. "I wanted to get those cattails just right," he told Giblin as the latter leafed in wonderment through a thick sheaf of reference sketches that the artist had made for just one of the illustrations in *The Tailypo* (1977), retold by his daughter, Joanna Galdone. Several years earlier, when the editor suggested an alternate pose for the goose in *Henny Penny* (1968), Galdone had replied without hesitation: "But Jim, a goose wouldn't do that, and I don't want children to think that it could."

Galdone, who was already in his mid-forties when he illustrated his first children's book, became one of the field's most prolific artists. From 1951 until his death in 1986, he illustrated an average of six books a year. Throughout, he maintained a keen sense of his audience. Although he turned for inspiration to the paintings, prints, and drawings of such old masters as Rembrandt, Goya, Hogarth, and Daumier, he made no pretense to creating picture-book art destined to hang in a museum. Contemporary media, especially the movies, influenced his approach to narrative pacing and to visual storytelling generally. Knowing that copies of his books were bound for use in preschool and elementary-school classrooms and public libraries, he planned his illustrations with the child in the last row at story hour in mind. Bold, posterlike images and layouts became hallmarks of his unfussy, deliberately accessible style.

So, too, did small, incidental details that only the child in a position to look very closely was likely to notice. Galdone assumed that young readers would make the effort. "I think children get [so] easily bored," he once wrote, "[that] there must be something in a [picture] book . . . that . . . they can discover for themselves." Often, that "something" takes the form of a wry comic touch: in *The Three Bears* (1972), for instance, Little Wee Bear's toy teddy—a fourth bear, to allow the third bear (and readers) to feel a little less small. Equally surprising in that book are Galdone's renderings of the principal characters: gap-toothed Goldilocks, who looks peppery enough to have been Eloise of the Plaza's country cousin, and the Bear family themselves, who in the opening scenes have such unexpectedly thoughtful looks in their eyes. What are they thinking? As the story unfolds, Galdone compels us to ask this while also putting readers in the truly fascinating position of feeling greater sympathy for a family of bears than for a spry but essentially insufferable fellow human.

Before turning to a career in illustration, Galdone had studied painting with the proto-abstract expressionist master Hans Hofmann and had come away convinced that abstraction "just wasn't for me." He later realized, however, that "abstraction is present in all good works of art." In Galdone's illustration, the abstract element turns up in such varied guises as the dramatic use of white space in *The Three Bears* (1972), the playful type treatments in *The Little Red Hen* (1973), and the rhythmical line work in *The Three Little Pigs* (1970).

As an illustrator, Galdone necessarily placed representation before abstraction. The subject that more than any other became the unifying thread of his varied and substantial body of work is the resilience and glory of nature. "I like to keep contact with nature in my art," he once told an interviewer, "whenever and wherever possible."

Nature mattered just as much to him in his everyday life. Galdone was a lifelong cat fancier, as can be readily gleaned from his sly, expressive drawings of feline folk in *The Little Red Hen* and *Cat Goes Fiddle-i-fee* (1985). Following World War II, during which he had served in the U.S. Army Corps of Engineers, he and his wife Jannelise left New York for rural Rockland County, northwest of the city. The couple later bought a Vermont farm as a summer home, where, in the meadows and woodlands on and around their property, Galdone spent happy, productive hours hiking, sketching, and just looking. Even as colder weather set in, he had trouble tearing himself away from the wildness and raw beauty of the place. "Can't leave the turning of the leaves to red just to tourists!" he wrote his editor in September 1972, as he prepared the finished artwork of *The Little Red Hen*. Earlier that summer he reported that Vermont had once again come through for him as inspiration: "I put the action [of *The Little Red Hen*] in an abandoned farm-house-type shack, but in proportion to the inhabitants. I'm so tired of cutesie-pie houses—and living up here now—I'm soaking up all delicious details of rural interiors—Animal [character]s can feel very cozy in dilapidated surroundings."

The decision to give a disheveled look to the animals' cottage was a characteristically subtle choice that highlights Galdone's affinity for animal tales with mordant comments to make on human nature. In *The Little Red Hen*, he gamely invites readers to think twice about why the cottage is such a mess. Is it simply because the hen's housemates never help out with the chores? Or might it also be that the brooder herself is really not quite the stiff-necked perfectionist she at first seems? What, after all, could be more cozy than the household's battered Victorian sofa—mismatched legs, sagging springs, and all? That earnest hen seems a little less prim—and a bit more human—just for living with such a rundown, but quintessentially homey, old thing on the premises.

A knowing acceptance of human frailties and contradictions lies at the heart of Galdone's tender but tough-minded picture books, many of which quickly became library, school, and household standards. Yet as an artist, Galdone, who received two Caldecott Honors—for *Anatole* (McGraw-Hill, 1956) and a year later for *Anatole and the Cat* (McGraw-Hill, 1957), both by Eve Titus—remained a restless spirit who always had it in mind to do a better job the next time around. "Today, . . . in fog, snow and drizzle I walked thru the woods again," he wrote his editor from Vermont in September 1976, "to get more into the outdoor scenes of Tailypo." Asked why the effort was worth it, he explained that he felt a special responsibility to children, to help them raise the level of their taste and to create art for the young that might stimulate their own art-making activities. And like the third little pig in the tale—the sole survivor, who wisely made his house of bricks—Galdone built to last. "[The pictures] one puts in a book . . . [are] SO final," he observed, with his usual mixture of heedfulness and hope—"and so satisfying if into this applied art form one can sneak in some things that will strike a chord."

Leonard S. Marcus

The Three Little Pigs

The THREE LITTLE PIGS

PAUL GALDONE

Once upon a time
there was an old sow with three little pigs.
She had no money to keep them,
so she sent them off to seek their fortune.

6

The first little pig met a man
with a bundle of straw,
and said to him:
"Please, man, give me that straw
to build me a house."

So the man did,
and the little pig
built his house with it.

Along came a wolf.

He knocked at the door, and said:

"Little pig, little pig, let me come in."

"No, no," said the little pig.

"Not by the hair of my chinny chin chin."

"Then I'll huff, and I'll puff,

and I'll blow your house in," said the wolf.

So the wolf huffed, and he puffed,
and he blew the house in.
And he ate up the first little pig.

The second little pig
met a man
with a bundle
of sticks,
and said:
"Please, man,
give me those sticks
to build me a house."

14

So the man did,
and the little pig built his house with them.

Then along came the wolf, and said:
"Little pig, little pig,
let me come in."

"No, no! Not by the hair
of my chinny chin chin."

"Then I'll huff, and I'll puff,
and I'll blow your house in,"
said the wolf.

So he huffed, and he puffed,
and he huffed and he puffed, and
at last he blew the house in.
And he ate up the second little pig.

The third little pig
met a man
with a load of bricks,
and said:
"Please, man,
give me those bricks
to build me a house."

So the man did,
and the little pig built his house with them.

Soon the same wolf came along,
and said:
"Little pig, little pig,
let me come in."

"No, no! Not by the hair
of my chinny chin chin."

"Then I'll huff, and I'll puff,
and I'll blow your house in,"
said the wolf.

Well, he huffed, and he puffed
and he huffed and he puffed
and he huffed and he puffed.

But he could *not* blow the house in.

At last the wolf stopped
huffing and puffing, and said:
"Little pig, I know where there is
a nice field of turnips."

"Where?" said the little pig.

"On Mr. Smith's farm," said the wolf.
"I will come for you tomorrow morning.
We will go together,
and get some turnips for dinner."

"Very well," said the little pig.
"What time will you come?"

"Oh, at six o'clock," said the wolf.

Well, the little pig got up at five.
He went to Mr. Smith's farm,
and got the turnips
before the wolf came to his house.

"Little pig, are you ready?" asked the wolf.

The little pig said, "Ready!

I have been and come back again

and I got a nice potful of turnips for my dinner."

The wolf was very angry.
But then he thought of another way
to get the little pig, so he said:
"Little pig, I know where
there is a nice apple tree."

"Where?" said the pig.

"Down at Merry Garden," replied the wolf.
"I will come for you
at five o'clock tomorrow morning
and we will get some apples."

Well, the little pig got up

the next morning at four o'clock,

and went off for the apples.

He wanted to get back home before the wolf came.

But it was a long way to Merry Garden,

and then he had to climb the tree.

Just as he was climbing back down

with his basket full of apples,

he saw the wolf coming!

"Little pig!" the wolf said.
"You got here before me!
Are the apples nice?"

"Yes, very," said the little pig.

"I will throw one down to you."

And he threw the apple as far as he could throw.

While the wolf ran to pick it up,

the little pig jumped down and ran home.

The next day the wolf came again
and said to the little pig: "Little pig, there is a fair
at Shanklin this afternoon. Would you like to go?"

"Oh, yes," said the little pig.
"When will you come to get me?"

"At three," said the wolf.

Well, the little pig went off at two o'clock
and bought a butter churn at the fair.

He was going home with it
when he saw the wolf coming!

The little pig jumped into the butter churn to hide.

The churn fell over and rolled
down the hill with the little pig in it.
This frightened the wolf so much
that he turned around and ran home.

Later the wolf went to the little pig's house
and told him what had happened.
"A great round thing came rolling down the hill
right at me," the wolf said.

"Hah, I frightened you then," said the little pig.
"I went to the fair and bought a butter churn.
When I saw you, I got into it,
and rolled down the hill."

The wolf was very angry indeed.
"I'm going to climb down your chimney
and eat you up!" he said.

When the little pig heard the wolf on the roof—

he hung a pot
full of water in the fireplace.
Then he built a blazing fire.
Just as the wolf was coming down the chimney,
the little pig took the cover off the pot,
and in fell the wolf.
The little pig quickly put the cover on again,
boiled up the wolf, and ate him for supper.

41

And the little pig lived happily ever afterward.

The Three Bears

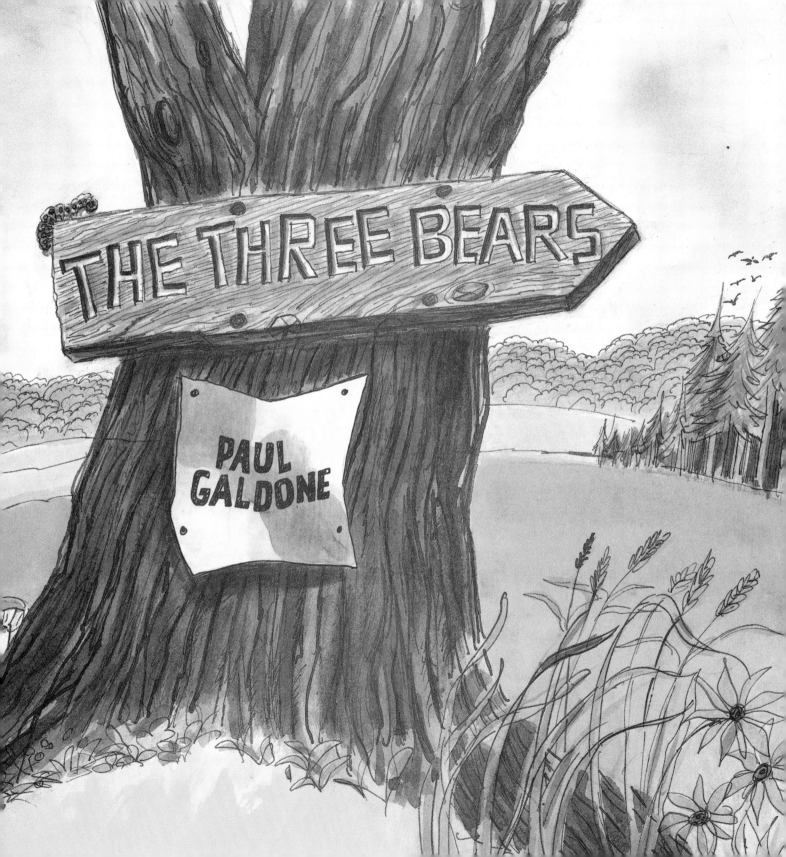

nce upon a time there were Three Bears who lived
together in a house of their own in the woods.

one was
a Middle-Sized Bear,

One of them was
a Little Wee Bear,

and the other was
a Great Big Bear.

49

They each had a bowl for their porridge.

The Little Wee Bear
had a little wee bowl,

the Middle-Sized Bear
had a middle-sized bowl,

and the Great Big Bear
had a great big bowl.

They each had a chair to sit in.

The Little Wee Bear
had a little wee chair,

the Middle-Sized Bear
had a middle-sized chair,

and the Great Big Bear
had a great big chair.

And they each had a bed to sleep in.

The Little Wee Bear had a little wee bed,

the Middle-Sized Bear had a middle-sized bed,

and the Great Big Bear had a great big bed.

One morning, the Three Bears
made porridge for breakfast
and poured it into their bowls.
But it was too hot to eat.
So they decided to go
for a walk in the woods
until it cooled.

While the Three Bears were walking,

a little girl named Goldilocks
came to their house.

54

First she looked in at the window,

and then she peeked through the keyhole.

Of course there was nobody inside.

Goldilocks turned the handle of the door.

The door was not locked, because
the Three Bears were trusting bears.
They did no one any harm, and never
thought anyone would harm them.

So Goldilocks opened the door and went right in.

There was the porridge
on the table.
It smelled very, very good!

Goldilocks didn't stop to think whose porridge it was.
She went straight to it.

First she tasted the porridge
of the Great Big Bear.
But it was too hot.

Then she tasted the porridge
of the Middle-Sized Bear.
But it was too cold.

Then she tasted the porridge
of the Little Wee Bear.

It was neither too hot nor too cold, but just right. Goldilocks liked it so much that she ate it all up.

Then Goldilocks went into the parlor to see what else she could find.

There were the three chairs.

First she sat down in the chair
of the Great Big Bear.
But it was too hard.

Then she sat down in the chair
of the Middle-Sized Bear.
But it was too soft.

Then she sat down in the chair
of the Little Wee Bear.
It was neither too hard
nor too soft, but just right.
Goldilocks liked it so much
that she rocked and rocked,

until . . .

60

the bottom of the chair fell out!

Down she went—plump!—onto the floor.

Goldilocks went into the bedroom
where the Three Bears slept.

First she lay down upon the bed
of the Great Big Bear.
But it was too high at the head for her.

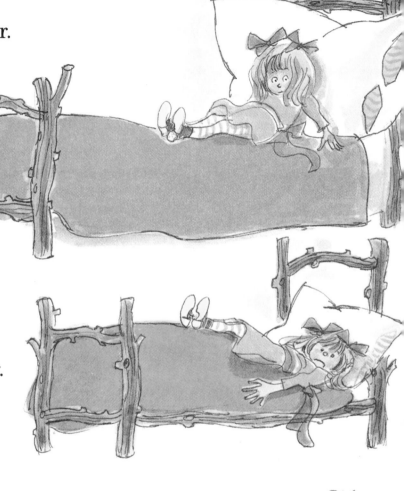

Then she lay down upon the bed
of the Middle-Sized Bear.
But it was too high at the foot for her.

Then she lay down upon the bed
of the Little Wee Bear.
It was neither too high at the head
nor too high at the foot, but just right.
Goldilocks liked it so much that
she covered herself up and fell fast asleep.

By this time,
the Three Bears thought
their porridge
would be cool enough.

So they came home
for breakfast.

Goldilocks had left
the spoon of the Great Big Bear
in his porridge bowl.
He noticed it, first thing.

"SOMEBODY HAS BEEN
TASTING MY PORRIDGE!"
said the Great Big Bear
in his great big voice.

Goldilocks had left
the spoon of the Middle-Sized Bear
in her porridge bowl, too.

"SOMEBODY HAS BEEN TASTING MY PORRIDGE!"
said the Middle-Sized Bear
in her middle-sized voice.

Then the Little Wee Bear looked at his bowl.

"SOMEBODY HAS BEEN TASTING MY PORRIDGE
AND HAS EATEN IT ALL UP!"
cried the Little Wee Bear
in his little wee voice.

The Three Bears went
into the parlor.

Then the Little Wee Bear looked at his chair.

"SOMEBODY HAS BEEN SITTING IN MY CHAIR
AND HAS SAT RIGHT THROUGH IT!"
cried the Little Wee Bear
in his little wee voice.

The Three Bears went into the bedroom.

Goldilocks had pulled the pillow
of the Great Big Bear out of place.
He noticed it, first thing.

"SOMEBODY HAS BEEN LYING IN MY BED!"
said the Great Big Bear in his great big voice.

Then the Little Wee Bear looked at his bed.

"SOMEBODY HAS BEEN LYING IN MY BED—AND HERE SHE IS!"
cried the Little Wee Bear in his little wee voice.

This woke Goldilocks up at once. There were the Three Bears
all staring at her.

73

Goldilocks was so frightened that
she tumbled out of bed and ran to the open window.

Out she jumped!

And she ran away as fast
as she could, never looking behind her.

No one knows what happened to Goldilocks after that.

As for the Three Bears, they never saw her again.

The Little Red Hen

The Little Red Hen

The Little Red Hen

PAUL GALDONE

O nce upon a time
a cat and a dog and a mouse
and a little red hen
all lived together in a cozy little house.

83

The cat liked to sleep all day
on the soft couch.

The dog liked to nap all day
on the sunny back porch.

And the mouse liked to snooze all day
in the warm chair by the fireside.

So the little red hen had to do all the housework.

She cooked the meals and washed the dishes
and made the beds. She swept the floor
and washed the windows
and mended the clothes.

She raked the leaves
and mowed the grass
and hoed the garden.

One day when she was hoeing the garden
she found some grains of wheat.

"Who will plant this wheat?"
cried the little red hen.

93

"Not I," said the mouse.

"Then I will," said the little red hen. And she did.

Each morning the little red hen watered the wheat
and pulled the weeds.

Soon the wheat pushed through the ground
and began to grow tall.

When the wheat was ripe,
the little red hen asked,
"Who will cut this wheat?"

"N⬤t I," said the cat.

"N⬤t I," said the dog.

"N⬤t I," said the mouse.

"Then I will," said the little red hen.
And she did.

When the wheat was all cut, the little red hen asked,
"Now, who will take this wheat to the mill
to be ground into flour?"

"Not I," said the cat.

"Not I," said the dog.

"Not I," said the mouse.

"Then I will," said the little red hen. And she did.

The little red hen returned from the mill
carrying a small bag of fine white flour.
"Who will make a cake from this fine white flour?"
asked the little red hen.

"Not I," said the cat.

"Not I," said the dog.

"Not I," said the mouse.

103

"Then I will," said the little red hen. And she did.

She gathered sticks and made a fire in the stove.
Then she took milk and sugar and eggs and butter
and mixed them in a big bowl
with the fine white flour.

When the oven was hot she poured
the cake batter into a shining pan
and put it in the oven.

Soon a delicious smell
filled the cozy little house.

The cat got off the soft couch
and strolled into the kitchen.

The dog got up from the sunny back porch
and came into the kitchen.

The mouse jumped down from his warm chair
and scampered into the kitchen.

The little red hen
was just taking
a beautiful cake
out of the oven.

111

"Who will eat this cake?"
asked the little red hen.

"I will!" cried the cat.
"I will!" cried the dog.
"I will!" cried the mouse.

113

But the little red hen said,

"All by myself
I planted the wheat,
I tended the wheat,
I cut the wheat,
I took the wheat to the mill
to be ground into flour.

All by myself
I gathered the sticks,
I built the fire,
I mixed the cake.
And
all by myself

I am going to eat it!"

And so she did,
to the very last crumb.

After that,

whenever there was work to be done,
the little red hen had three very eager helpers.

Cat Goes Fiddle-i-fee

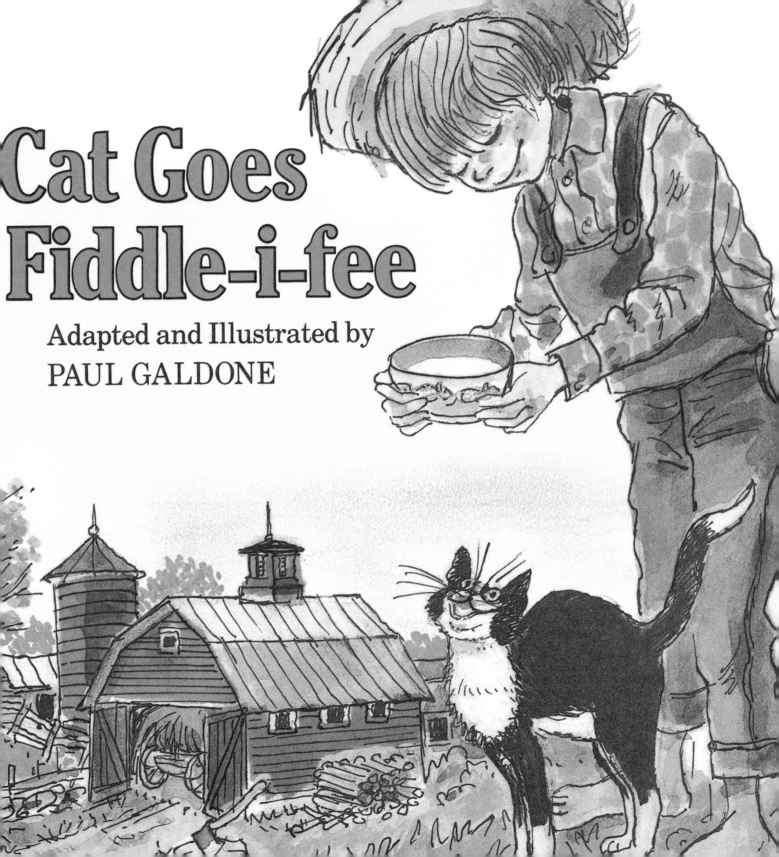

Cat Goes Fiddle-i-fee

Adapted and Illustrated by
PAUL GALDONE

I had a cat and the cat pleased me,
I fed my cat by yonder tree.

122

Cat goes fiddle-i-fee.

I had a hen and the hen pleased me,
I fed my hen by yonder tree.

Hen goes chimmy-chuck, chimmy-chuck,
Cat goes fiddle-i-fee.

I had a duck and the duck pleased me,
I fed my duck by yonder tree.

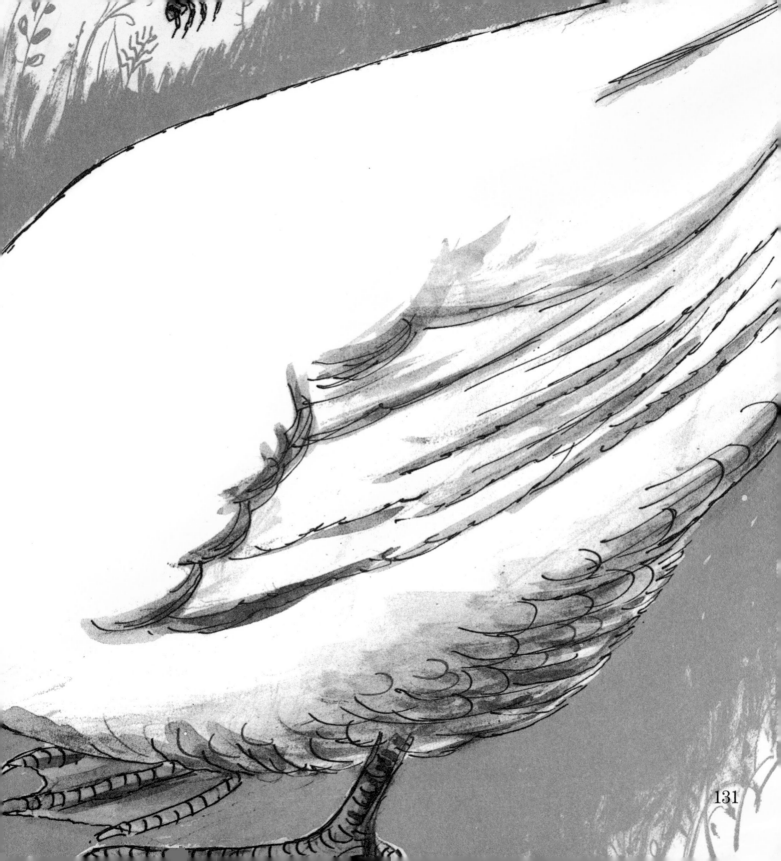

Duck goes quack, quack,

Hen goes chimmy-chuck, chimmy-chuck,

Cat goes fiddle-i-fee.

I had a goose and the goose pleased me,
I fed my goose by yonder tree.

Goose goes swishy, swashy,

Duck goes quack, quack,

Hen goes chimmy-chuck, chimmy-chuck,

Cat goes fiddle-i-fee.

I had a sheep and the sheep pleased me,
I fed my sheep by yonder tree.

Sheep goes baa, baa,
Goose goes swishy, swashy,
Duck goes quack, quack,
Hen goes chimmy-chuck, chimmy-chuck,
Cat goes fiddle-i-fee.

I had a pig and the pig pleased me,
I fed my pig by yonder tree.

Pig goes griffy, gruffy,
Sheep goes baa, baa,
Goose goes swishy, swashy,
Duck goes quack, quack,
Hen goes chimmy-chuck, chimmy-chuck,
Cat goes fiddle-i-fee.

I had a cow and the cow pleased me,
I fed my cow by yonder tree.

Cow goes moo, moo,
Pig goes griffy, gruffy,
Sheep goes baa, baa,
Goose goes swishy, swashy,
Duck goes quack, quack,
Hen goes chimmy-chuck, chimmy-chuck,
Cat goes fiddle-i-fee.

I had a horse and the horse pleased me,
I fed my horse by yonder tree.

Horse goes neigh, neigh,
Cow goes moo, moo,
Pig goes griffy, gruffy,
Sheep goes baa, baa,
Goose goes swishy, swashy,
Duck goes quack, quack,
Hen goes chimmy-chuck, chimmy-chuck,
Cat goes fiddle-i-fee.

I had a dog and the dog pleased me,
I fed my dog by yonder tree.

Dog goes bow-wow, bow-wow,
Horse goes neigh, neigh,
Cow goes moo, moo,
Pig goes griffy, gruffy,
Sheep goes baa, baa,
Goose goes swishy, swashy,
Duck goes quack, quack,
Hen goes chimmy-chuck, chimmy-chuck,
Cat goes fiddle-i-fee.

Then Grandma came
and she fed me . . .

while the others dozed
by yonder tree.

And cat went fiddle-i-fee.